A Queen in the Garden

Story by Heather Hammonds
Illustrations by Robert Dunn

Contents

Chapter 1

Bees in the Tree!

It was Saturday morning, and the sun was shining.

"Let's go out into the garden,"
Nina said to her brother, Tino.

"Yes," said Tino. "We can have our snacks
in our playhouse."

Nina and Tino went outside.
Their playhouse was near a big tree.

Suddenly, Nina heard a buzzing noise.
"Oh, no!" she cried.
"Look at all the bees in the tree."

There were thousands of honey bees
flying around a tree branch.

"We have to tell Grandpa!" shouted Tino.

They rushed back inside.

"Those bees are looking for a new home," said Grandpa, when he saw the tree branch.

"They might sting us," said Nina.

"The bees won't sting you if you stay away from them," said Grandpa.

Grandpa told Tino and Nina to stay inside.

"My friend Pia is a beekeeper," he said. "I'll call her and ask her to help us."

"Grandpa, can we please go on the internet and find out about bees?" asked Tino.

"Yes," said Grandpa.

"Every bee hive has a queen bee,"
said Nina, looking at the computer.
"The queen lays thousands of tiny bee eggs."

"When a bee hive gets full of bees,
the queen flies away with some of them,
to find a new home," Tino read.

"Grandpa was right," said Nina.
"The bees in our garden
are looking for a new home!"

Chapter 2

Help from a Beekeeper

At twelve o'clock, Pia the beekeeper came to Tino and Nina's house.

"I'll catch these bees and move them into a new hive at my farm," she said.

Pia put on a bee suit
so the bees couldn't sting her.
Then she went into the garden with a big box.

Pia shook most of the bees
off the tree branch and they fell into the box.

"Some bees are still flying towards you," Tino called out.

"Yes," called Pia.
"But the queen is in the box, so they will follow her into it."

Soon, Pia put the lid on the box and took the bees to her van.

"Would you like to visit your bees next week?" she asked.

"Yes, please!" shouted Tino and Nina.

Chapter 3

A Visit to the Bee Hives

The next Saturday,
Grandpa drove Tino and Nina to Pia's farm.

Pia helped everyone to put on bee suits,
and they went to see the bees.

Tino and Nina saw the bees
going in and out of their new bee hive.

Pia showed them her other bee hives, too.

Then she gave them a jar of honey
that her bees had made!

After Tino and Nina went home, Grandpa made them some toast with honey from Pia's bees.

"I'm glad a queen came to our garden," said Nina.

"I am, too," said Tino, smiling.